To Freya

Sending hugs

Love

Auntie Julia and Anya

Faraday Bear & Friends
Goodbye Mother Bear

First published in 2021
Copyright © 2021 Adam D. Searle

Written by Adam D. Searle
Illustrated by Ian R. Ward
Designed by Stephanie Drake

ISBN (HARDBACK) : 978-1-9162985-2-1
ISBN (PAPERBACK) : 978-1-9162985-4-5
ISBN (eBook) : 978-1-9162985-3-8

www.adamdsearle-author.com

FARADAY BEAR & FRIENDS

Goodbye Mother Bear

Illustrated by
Ian R. Ward

Written by
Adam D. Searle

It can be hard sometimes to say goodbye.

Especially if you were never to see that person again.

Faraday Bear never had the chance to say goodbye to his mother; he thought that she would get better again.

And that she would return home.

But she never did.

Faraday thought that nobody really understood how he felt. But when he went back to school, he found his teacher was very kind to him.

His friends also did their best. They had been told about his loss by their own parents and by the teacher at school, and they had greeted him nicely upon his return.

But he noticed that they reacted in different ways towards him. Some were very emotional and could not look him in the eyes when they spoke. Some avoided him altogether. Others tried to carry on as normal by getting him involved in playing games with them.

They even had a small football match.

But Faraday still felt very alone, he missed his mother and did not think his friends knew how he was feeling or knew how to make him feel better.

He was suffering from grief, and there were days when he felt so bad that he wanted to talk to no one and just to be left on his own.

He also felt angry and confused, and he would lose his temper just as easily as his friend Flint often did. He shouted at his father for not cooking him dinners like his mother used to, and for sending him to school when he did not want to go. Faraday understood that his father did this so he could be amongst his friends and for him to get involved in things and to start to recover.

And on his very bad days he would shout out angrily at those who wanted to help.

"Will you just leave me alone?" Faraday would snap.

He did not mean to hurt his friends; he did not understand that they too shared his pain for most had known his mother well.

He felt angry that his mother was gone. It had left a huge hole in his life and his home now felt empty. He could not tell his friends or his father how angry, lonely and cheated he felt. There was nobody he could blame.

And he hated it when he felt sad, and he struggled not to cry in front of anyone. Especially his father who was also grieving. But, despite his outbursts, his friends helped by being there for Faraday.

And, no one knew how he felt more than Jack Badger, who was new to school and the village of Woodland Green.

"My father passed away last year." He told Faraday one lunch time after finding the bear sitting alone under a tree. "I live with my step- mum and half -siblings."

"Where's your mum?" Faraday asked.

"She passed away when I was very young," Jack explained. Faraday was surprised by how Jack spoke of his parents with fondness, rather than sorrow, which is what he felt. He asked,

"How can you talk about them without getting upset?"

"Because they are still a part of me," Jack told him. "I am their son and I feel them every day in my heart."

And, as the days passed into weeks; and the weeks into months, Faraday found himself slowly healing. He no longer cried into his pillow at bedtime.

Nor did he get upset when he spoke about his mother, or stared at her framed picture.

In fact, talking about her made him feel a lot better, so that was what he and Jack often did.

Other times Faraday told his new friend about his father burning the morning toast or forgetting to put the dinner in the oven, while Jack told him about adjusting to his new life at school.

The two became good friends and Faraday was soon back getting involved into his schooling and activities. He often helped out his friends with their problems and troubles. Such as when Rex tore his shirt or Flint got angry at someone.

But Faraday still felt upset that he had never said goodbye to his mother. One day he spoke to his teacher, Mr Antler about this.

"Maybe you need to set up a memorial for her," Mr Antler suggested.

"What is a memorial?" Faraday asked.

"A memorial is something you make in the memory of a person." The teacher explained. "It can be something that they liked or loved and you keep it in their memory."

Faraday Bear thought this was a very good idea. He thanked his teacher and hurried out to find Jack.

"I am going to build a memorial for my mum." He told his friend. "So, I can say goodbye to her."

Jack also thought it was a very good idea.

After school that very day; after changing out of his school clothes and hungrily devouring a sandwich, he set of down to the woodlands. There, he came to a shallow stream which used to flow through the woods and out across the fields and down the hill to join the river.

Faraday followed the stream down to the edge of the woodlands where there was a field where his mum used to take him when he was young. She used to sit on a blanket as he played, either splashing or paddling about in the stream or climbing a tree. But, a few years ago, during a storm, an old, dead tree had fallen across the stream at the edge of the woodlands. Rocks, mud and vegetation had gathered against the tree, and the ground was very wet and boggy where the water had pooled up. Now only a thin trickle of water seeped down the streambed towards where the river flowed at the bottom of the hill at the edge of the village.

Faraday came to where the tree lay, dead and rotting across the stream, surrounded with rocks and dirt. He clambered down and started to lift and heave rocks and stones to either side. He soon got his dungarees wet and muddy, but the little bear did not care.

Shortly his friends appeared along with Jack, who had told them of his plan.

"What are you doing?" Rex Alsatian asked.

"My mum used to love sitting on the green field beside the stream." Faraday said.

"She used to sit there while I would play. Now, I am going to clear this all so the stream flows just as it used to. It will be my memorial to her."

"Then let us help you." Flint said, leaping down with a splash on the other side of the fallen tree.

"Yes, we will help." Charmer Cat said, and jumped in. She was followed by her twin brother, Chase.

At first Faraday was upset because this was something that he wanted to do himself. But his friends insisted, for they had all had known his mother rather well.

"Rex has bought his dads gardening tools." Spike Hedgehog said.

"A scout always comes prepared," the pup declared happily. They all got to work, including Jack. He had never known Faraday's mother, but helped out of respect for his friend.

They worked together, lifting heavy rocks and boulders, clearing away leaves and foliage, branches and twigs. Soon they were all as wet and muddy as Faraday, including Mandy Mouse, who hated getting wet.

The tree was so rotten that it broke up into wet soggy clumps. The water gushed through the space they had made, flowing out and over their legs. The sound was like music to Faraday's ears.

"We did it!" Mandy Mouse squeaked and everybody cheered.

"This is just how I remember it," Felix Fox smiled.

Wet and muddy the friends followed Faraday as he stepped out of the stream and onto the field where Mother Bear always used to sit.

"But why do you look so sad, Faraday?" Chase asked. He was concerned about his friend. "Is it not what you wanted?"

"It is perfect in every way." Faraday confessed sadly. "I was hoping that by doing this I would feel better. But I still feel bad that I did not get to say goodbye to her."

"Maybe you still can." Jack said. "As this place means such a lot to you and your mother this is an ideal place to say goodbye." The others were confused.

"How?" Rex asked.

"We shall meet back here one day when Faraday is ready and I will show you how."

In time, on a mild evening, Faraday, his father and friends, met on the green by the stream.

With his father's help, Faraday dug a hole near the spot where his mother used to sit and planted a tree.

His father had said a tree would be a great memorial. Faraday agreed, and had chosen an apple tree because apples had been his mother's favourite fruit.

Jack told Faraday what to do to say his goodbye, and he gave him a notepad and pen.

Faraday wrote his goodbye down on a sheet of paper, tore it out of the pad, and folded it up many times until it became a paper boat. He took a small square photo of his mum and slipped it inside of the boat.

Faraday could not help but shed a tear as he crouched down beside the stream and placed the boat onto the water. He could

not help feeling his chest burn with emotion.
A lump formed in his throat.

The little bear was no longer afraid of showing his emotions
when he was among his good friends.

Faraday released the boat and watched as it bobbed away along
the stream and towards where the evening sun was sinking
down to the horizon.

High above them the first stars peered down watchfully as the little bear stood among his friends.

"Goodbye mum," He whispered as the boat sailed out of sight into the distance.

"Goodbye, Mother Bear." His friends said under the sky of watchful stars.

Goodbye, Mother Bear.

The end

Printed in Great Britain
by Amazon

20200625R00022